Passing Through the Dream...

by
Rebecca Masterton

LIGHT READING

Published by Light Reading
PO Box 59164
London NW2 9HF
www.light-reading.co.uk

ISBN 978-0-9559344-0-7

Jacket design by Mukhtar Sanders
www.inspiraldesign.com

Photograph by Rebecca Masterton

Printed by Imprint Digital
www.imprintdigital.net

Contents

Nobody knew what had happened to the plane. There was no evidence of it having been shot down. It had simply disappeared off the radar on its way back to Washington, with Donald Rumsfeld in it. The last place it had been detected was over Siwa, the western desert of Egypt. Then after that, it had vanished from the flight controllers' screens. Of course, today it was big news. Everybody was panicking, puzzled, not sure what to do. There were rumblings in Washington that perhaps Cairo should be carpet-bombed, as a way of persuading any potential militants to own up. Wiping out faceless brown people was always a satisfying, if short-term, panacea for the outrage that anyone should dare to touch the temporal rulers of the material realm.

However, there were also rumours that Rumsfeld had simply had enough; or rather, he had become bored. Even after more than five hundred thousand Iraqi deaths (caused by sanctions, war, etc.) those damn Arabs were *still* being ungrateful for having been saved. When were they *ever* going to be beaten into submission and gratitude? But more importantly, when were the oil revenues going to start trickling into his bank accounts? The price of oil had gone up, not down. And then there was the tedium of having to churn out the religio-political ideology in order to placate restless voters. Was it all really worth it?

Rumsfeld's colleagues were interviewed. Had he shown any signs of depression before leaving for Iraq? Bush answered that he had in fact been a little annoyed for not managing to get his favourite suit back from the cleaners before setting off. Rice said that he had not been making his usual satirical jokes about Bush's illiteracy over morning coffee. Yes, he had seemed quieter than usual. Cheney had noticed that, during a round of golf, Rumsfeld's ball had got lost in the sandpit and he had failed to find it, even after twenty minutes of digging in the sand with his golf-club. Perhaps this was a portent from the Heavens about his disappearance. It was difficult to tell exactly *what* he had been thinking, or *how* he had been feeling, before he set off for Iraq, but then it always was difficult to tell. Those steely, close-set eyes lurking behind deceptively benign round spectacles gave away nothing personal whatsoever.

Blair appeared on television, hands pressed together as if in prayer, making a very good speech about how concerned he was about Rumsfeld's disappearance. He put all the weighty pauses in the right places, and now and again his voice cracked, effectively creating the impression of a person who had sincere feelings. Rumsfeld, he said, had always shown compassion for the Iraqi people and had done his best to ensure that the whole world was liberated. It was inconceivable that he would abandon his mission half-way. He was, after all, a man of principle. He would continue to the bitter end, no matter how many had to die.

Black Hawk helicopters were sent out to search the Siwa desert for signs of a plane crash. They found nothing. The Mediterranean was scanned using infra-red radar. Nothing was found, except the remains of one or two Greek ships, sunk off the coast of Carthage after Aeneas had abandoned Dido. This was the strange thing: if Rumsfeld had been kidnapped by those pesky Bedouins, there would surely remain the wreckage of the plane. They could not simply bury it under the sand. Anyway, infra-red radar showed no signs of any wreckage, and raiding Bedouin tents brought no joy either, particularly since Bedouins did not understand much English, even when it was shouted at top volume.

After the plane had failed to be found in Siwa, the whole of the Middle East came under suspicion and Bush made a speech about how the dark clouds of Armageddon were gathering on the horizon; and how soon, if Rumsfeld was not handed over, the rivers of the Nile, the Euphrates and any others in the area, would be running with blood.

"The people who have taken Rumsfeld hate freedom", said Bush. "But we'll get them, no matter what it takes. We will leave no grain of sand unturned in our search for Rumsfeld."

Speculation spread to the possibility that Rumsfeld might never have boarded the plane in the first place and that the plane had done a U-turn and gone back to Iraq, because it had taken off without him; but some soldiers said that they definitely saw him board, and they definitely saw that plane take off, and it was definitely in the direction of America. Prayers and vigils were held for Rumsfeld's return. Bishops and priests made speeches. Bush said he would continue with his mission, even without Rumsfeld, and he was sure that Rumsfeld would be proud of him. He spoke with tears in his eyes and his voice cracked, effectively creating the impression of a person who had sincere feelings.

Washington wanted to bomb Cairo, Damascus, Tehran and any other city in the area, in order to put pressure on the Egyptian, Syrian and Iranian governments to hand Rumsfeld over. France objected, saying that diplomatic pressure must be exerted first, and that anyway, perhaps members of the US government should just accept that Rumsfeld was not going to come back, and get on with their lives. At least that was one global irritant off the list. The newspapers were filled with vitriol, both for Rumsfeld and those barbaric fanatics who must have carried him off. Stock markets see-sawed, soaring one minute and plunging the next. People in Texas felt insecure and looked to Bush to do something, and Bush said, "I will do something." In many other parts of the world, however, a mood of tranquillity could be felt in the streets. People began to smile again. Others said that, perhaps there was hope, after all.

Seven days passed and there was still no sign of him, but we knew where he was. We had invited him, quietly, to a place which does not exist on earth, because those of our spiritual lineage were concerned, and because this is the way that we work. Do not think that our leaders do not act, even though they left this realm fourteen hundred years ago. They did not die for nothing.

Somebody spotted Donald Rumsfeld at a stall in an outdoor market, in Dakar, Senegal. We had given him some money, but by the time he was seen, he had spent it all, since he had taken a liking to jollof rice and plantain, and enjoyed sitting on the steps of the local mosque in the evenings, sharing a plateful with the imam and a few of the Tijani brothers. A reporter for *The Washington Post*, who was in town to research Senegal's new *zakāt* law, saw a tall, white man with mousy brown hair, round glasses and a fairly long beard. He was wearing a long white *jubba* and wide trousers. As the reporter passed this man, he heard his voice, and instantly recognised the slightly high-pitched twang, as Rumsfeld begged the market woman to spare him a few plantains.

The reporter instantly punched in the number for *The Washington Post* office on his satellite mobile, and, in the middle of the crowded market, exactly two feet away from Rumsfeld, shouted,

"Guess what! I've found Rumsfeld! No, no! I'm serious! I don't know how he got here. Yeah, he seems OK. Er… he's just negotiating a plantain deal at the moment… I –"

Rumsfeld turned, a flood of emotion filling his heart, for it seemed like years since he had heard an American voice.

***

Kennedy Airport was packed to bursting with reporters and photographers. Rumsfeld had been found and he was going to touchdown on the tarmac any second. The air was hot with speculation. Had he been tortured, beaten and starved? Had he managed to escape his captors? Or had he, after all, just gone on holiday for a while?

The plane touched down and drew to a halt. Immediately it was lit up with spotlights. A set of steps was brought to the plane door. The crowd murmured in anticipation. The plane door opened, and there, blinking in the spotlights, was a man they did not recognise. At first they cheered, but the cheers quickly died out and a hubbub of confusion rose into the warm night air.

"Hey! He looks like one of those Musslums!"

"Look at what they've done to him! My God! I wonder if he's OK?"

Rumsfeld grinned awkwardly and staggered down the steps, bodyguards fighting off the crowd. Reporters launched themselves in his direction, forcing their microphones towards him. He took a few steps, then stopped. The reporters sensed that he was going to speak. Pictures of Rumsfeld with a beard and dressed in white were flashed around the world, and then, unbelievably, he said,

"Ash-hadu an-lā ilāha illallahu, wa ash-hadu anna Muhammad Rasulullah."

The crowd thought he must have gone mad. They uttered exclamations of dismay, but there just so happened to be a Muslim reporter in the crowd, and he shouted out, above the noise,

"Mr Rumsfeld, have you really become Muslim?"

"Guys", said Rumsfeld, "I cannot explain to you what I have seen and what I have been through. I have met representatives of the Prophet Muhammad himself, peace and blessings be upon him and his family. I have also been privileged to meet the Prophet Muhammad, peace and blessings be upon him and his family. One of his representatives took out my heart and showed it to me. It was like a little lump of granite. Then he blew on it and recited some verses from the Qur'an, and I saw my heart turn into a lump of flesh, and that lump of flesh had a light inside it. They put my heart back into my chest. They introduced me to some of the Prophet's faithful companions, may God have mercy on them, and also to his family. This is a family of knowledge, people. You would not believe how I have cried."

"Mr Rumsfeld! Mr Rumsfeld!" everybody shouted at once. "Mr Rumsfeld, what are you going to do now, Mr Rumsfeld? This is political suicide! You must be crazy!"

"People", said Rumsfeld, "I was crazy and now I am sane, or let's say, saner. Once you taste the sacred you can't forget it. And once you see the history in things, and the meaning in things, you can't carry on unless you are just plain stupid, and I have always liked to think of myself as an intelligent man."

"But Mr Rumsfeld! What are you going to do now?"

"It goes without saying that I am resigning from the US government, as that kind of power makes me feel *sick*. My guts can't tolerate it. And I'm going to do my best to become ever more conscious of the Divine. And I'm going to do my best to campaign against the oppression inflicted on the world by our country, the United States and by other countries such as Britain and Russia. I'm not just campaigning for Muslims; I'm campaigning for the folks of South America whose economies have been sent down the plughole by our policies; I'm campaigning for the Palestinians, Christian and Muslim; I'm giving away all the cash I've acquired through arms deals with Saddam Hussein and Africa and Indonesia and places like that; I'm campaigning for greater justice for the American people: those who have been prevented from voting because of our manipulations of the law; I'm campaigning for the better treatment of prisoners around the world, including ours, who are routinely tortured using methods you've seen in Abu Ghraib; I'm campaigning against the US government's funding of terrorists, such as the Mujahedeen, who have killed and blown up thousands of ordinary Muslims in Iran; I'm campaigning against the rigging of elections in Afghanistan; I'm campaigning for reparations to be made to the Somali people who were tortured and beaten by UN soldiers during that dirty war; I'm campaigning for blood money to be paid to the families of the five hundred thousand babies who have died as a result of UN sanctions and the depleted uranium that our missiles have spread about; I'm campaigning for the Burmese people whose family members have been raped and murdered on a US oil pipeline project; I'm campaigning for an end to tacit US support for temporal regimes around the world that leave the people to sink into filth and poverty."

"But Mr Rumsfeld, aren't you afraid you might be assassinated by the CIA now?"

Before Rumsfeld could answer, a large white van with blacked-out windows pulled up behind him, and some men in long white coats leaped out on to the runway. Rushing towards him and taking him by the arms, they bundled him in to the van. He was never seen again.

Being on Time

Maurice de Jour had been working on his masterpiece for about seventeen years. This was the work that would make his name. He had decided to call it *Being on Time*. It was a post-modern amalgamation of transcendental phenomenology, existentialism and deconstructionism. These were no longer the days of Heidegger and Sartre; these were the days of MC Solaar and Mathieu Kassovitz. In other words, philosophy was no longer at the Sorbonne; it had dispersed into the streets, mixing with an assortment of historical fragments, which Maurice liked to call 'fragments of time'.

In order to be able to have some peace and finish his project, Maurice was spending his sabbatical in London: West Hampstead, to be precise – that charming corner of the city where one could still go to a café for a civilised cup of coffee and a read of the papers before commencing work. Of course, he had noticed that it was only a five-minute cab ride from there to the not-so-salubrious Kilburn High Road. Its multitude of tat-filled shops, bursting with crowds from every corner of the world, made him frown with consternation, if not fascination. It was a side of life he preferred not to see: cheap, garishly-coloured imported goods for those who could not afford more. It was also a symbol of an age in which the social and economic order had, in his opinion, gone tragically awry, threatening the very substance of existence.

Maurice wanted to bring philosophy back to where it belonged: to the realm of great thinkers; of changers of civilisation; of men who knew the art of rhetoric. Not that his intention was simply to make a rehash of ancient Greek values. No. What he wanted was to reinterpret those values in a contemporary way, so that they could be applied in any place and at any time – apart from Kilburn High Road on a Saturday morning.

He had found the perfect place at which to write: a room in a small hotel, whose bay windows overlooked a front garden filled with white rose bushes. When he went out at noon for breakfast, after a long night's work, the sight and scent of the roses inspired in him a sense of tranquillity and a strange yearning that he could not understand, and quickly repressed.

At night, the hours flew by. He sat at a desk at the window, the glow of the computer screen illuminating the ceiling. Only one table lamp was on. Next to him was a cold cup of coffee.

"Gadamer seeks to escape the finitude of existence through historical methodology", he wrote, "but historical methodology can only remain a methodology, a projection of the intellect on to an existence which remains finite."

In the silence of the room, as he contemplated his next sentence, he heard something which sounded very like a sigh. Thinking that perhaps

11

his jacket had slipped to the floor, he turned, irritated at the interruption, to find a tall, weary-looking African man in a green suit, sitting slightly slouched in the little armchair in the corner of the room. The man looked as if he might have been asleep. Certainly his eyelids were closed. Assuming him to be a hotel guest who had strayed through the wrong door, but uncertain of his temperament, Maurice cautiously stood up and slowly turned to face him, but the man remained motionless, his long, slender legs pressed with knees awkwardly together.

Maurice coughed. At this, the man suddenly opened his eyes, which startled Maurice with their powerful, unflinching gaze.

"I do apologise", said Maurice in French.

"I was not asleep", the man replied, also in French, and it was then that, remembering he was in England, Maurice realised he did not have an ordinary situation on his hands, although, for some strange reason, he adopted a manner of scrupulous politeness.

"Ah, ha-ha-ha", he laughed stiffly. "We both speak French. Well, well."

"Indeed", said the man, less amused.

"You do realise, don't you", said Maurice, "that this is actually my room. Perhaps you have it confused with yours?"

"Not at all", replied the man with disconcerting composure. "I came for a particular reason to see you. How is your wife?"

12

At this, Maurice, who had been smiling in order to show that he was a reasonable man, felt an inexplicable rage well up inside him and his instinct was to shout at his guest, to order him to get out immediately.

"Who are you? Are you a spy? I demand to know!" he shouted, hands trembling.

In fact, his wife had died nearly a year earlier from alcohol poisoning, although he told everyone that it had been cancer.

This time, it was his guest's turn to smile. He stood up, towering over Maurice by about six inches, and held out his hand.

"Allow me to introduce myself: I am Shaykh Amadou Thiam. My grandfather knew your grandfather, many years ago."

"What? That's nonsense!" scoffed Maurice. "My grandfather was an eminent doctor and scientist. How could he have known your grandfather? Why, he had never even set foot in Africa!"

"He didn't have to", replied Shaykh Amadou simply, "for my grandfather had spent a considerable amount of time in France. Actually, he is buried there."

"What was he doing in France?" demanded Maurice incredulously. "France cannot have had any business with him, that's for certain."

"He was in the army", said Shaykh Amadou, "fighting your war against Germany. You must surely know of the great debt that your country owes to my country, in this respect?"

"In the army", echoed Maurice. "What was he doing – helping to load up the pack horses?"

"Oh no", answered Shaykh Amadou, unperturbed by Maurice's goading. "He worked alongside your grandfather as a field doctor. They were great friends. He used to mention your grandfather a lot in his letters: what good work your grandfather was doing; how many lives he had saved."

"Yes", said Maurice proudly, "he was a great man, my grandfather. He almost died at the Battle of Ypres, trying to rescue a young foot soldier who was drowning in a bomb crater. The lad nearly dragged him down, you see. He was in hospital for a long time after that – shrapnel wounds and pneumonia. They awarded him a medal for bravery."

"Yes I know, for it was my grandfather who pulled him out of the bomb crater, although unfortunately the young foot soldier had already drowned", said Shaykh Amadou.

Maurice stared at Shaykh Amadou in astonishment. Then he sneered, "You're making it up."

"Why should I do that? Anyway, I have newspaper articles and photographs to prove it, showing my grandfather wearing his medal, which mysteriously disappeared after he was killed in the trenches", said Shaykh Amadou.

Maurice pursed his lips and narrowed his eyes. "Are you insinuating…?"

"I am not insinuating anything. I have simply come to ask for my grandfather's medal to be returned."

Maurice suddenly could no longer look Shaykh Amadou in the face. His eyes fell to the floor and shifted from side to side. It was true that, unlike Shaykh Amadou, he had no official photographs of his grandfather wearing the medal, just a few family snaps taken in the early 'sixties, shortly before his grandfather died. Then he hesitated. Supposing this man *was* making it all up? Supposing he was a con-artist?

"How do I know that you are who you say you are? You seem to know something of my family history, but you didn't know that my wife had died, did you?"

"Oh, I do beg your pardon", said Shaykh Amadou. "I did not mean your second wife – I meant your first wife. I assumed you must be in contact with her, because of your sons."

Maurice felt something cold enter his heart. He had guarded the secret of his first marriage and the existence of two sons, whom he had not seen for twenty years, with the zealous determination of a man who could not for one second afford to have cracks in his reputation. He was the celebrated Maurice de Jour, honoured and respected among his peers for his great insights into humanity and human destiny. That he had failed to maintain contact with his children for all those years was not something he desired to advertise.

"I have not seen that woman, or my sons, for more than twenty years", he growled. "Is that what you are here for, eh? To dig the dirt? It's none of your business – "

"Your eldest son, Pierre, has my grandfather's medal", interrupted Shaykh Amadou. "I merely thought that you could persuade him to give it up to its rightful owner."

Yes, Pierre had always loved the medal when he was little boy.

"And how am I to do that? I don't even know where he is, for goodness' sake!"

"I will have to leave that to you. He is your son", said Shaykh Amadou softly. "And now I have to go. I have a large community to take care of back home. I will return when you have retrieved the medal."

"Back home? You mean in Africa?"

"Yes", replied Shaykh Amadou faintly. "I am a busy man. I have many responsibilities."

Imagining the relief he would feel once he had shown the *shaykh* out, Maurice glanced in anticipation at the door, only to notice that it was locked from the inside, just has he had left it. He began to quiver. Shaykh Amadou looked at him and chuckled.

"You don't know about *burūz*, do you?"
"*Burūz?*"

"The ability to be in more than one place at once. You don't know about that, do you?"

Maurice was unable to answer. He suddenly felt horribly small. The *shaykh* chuckled again, and as he did so, he grew transparent, his voice seeming to vanish into the distance, with the simple words: *"A bientôt, mon ami"*. Then he was gone. Maurice stared at the empty space before him and realised that a lifetime's theories and a lifetime's work had just evaporated. He wondered whether he was mad, having a breakdown or had really seen what he had seen. He realised, with a terrible fear, that he was sane. And then he thought about his sons and he heard himself utter, in a strange kind of whisper, the word "Pierre".

It was when everything began to get out of hand that Arifa decided she had lived long enough. She realised that there was just no stopping the bloodshed. When it came down to it, they must get a kick out of killing each other, otherwise, why would they do it? For as long as mankind had existed, people had always thought that extermination was the solution. One would have thought they would have learned by now, but no, they generated only darkness upon darkness.

What made the world so mad was that everybody was shouting all at once and nobody was listening. Not only that: everybody was dividing into tribes. Missiles flew from one side; missiles flew from the other. Where was the sacred journey of the soul? Where was the beatific vision?

The code of the warrior had sunk into a sea of mud and blood. The practice of maintaining a warrior's stillness of mind had been replaced by a policy of caking prisoners in excrement. Respect for the enemy had now become putting the enemy on a dog-lead. Ugliness abounded.

"And yet, one has to go on living", thought Arifa, as she stared into the darkness.

At this moment, she was dead to the world – not in a suicidal sense – she had simply resigned, clocked out internally, turned away from the bad taste, the rotten smell.

"I am ready to leave now, thank you."

That night her soul visited the *barzakh*. Three spirits were sitting in a room. They smiled at her and said "Welcome to the spirit realm. Do you like it here?"

"Yes I do", she replied, without hesitation; but she had to go back to the lower realm, to continue to live.

Being dead to the world meant that, when she was driving, she wasn't really driving; when she was attending meetings, she wasn't really attending. There was comfort in the spring blossoms and the bird song, because that was a reminder of what lay beyond.

Being dead to the world, she noticed those who struggled to be in it: the frail, lost-looking Irishman with watery eyes and a bendy leg; the teenage boy with his cap turned backwards, walking like Charlie Chaplin in a failing attempt to be cool like his friends; the Sudanese lady anxiously looking out from behind the counter of a shop that was empty of customers.

It was just after the July bombings in London and there was a strange atmosphere in the city – strange, because everybody was trying to appear relaxed, while an undercurrent of tension manifested itself in nervous glances and silent, appeasing gestures. An avalanche of putrid darkness had been released upon the city. Arifa tried not to feel like a walking stereotype as she hurried to work, past the East London mosque. Today, there happened to be a BNP demonstration outside. More darkness. She decided to cross the road before she came too close to the demonstration, which seemed to be led by large, Germanic-looking men in heavy jackets and shades. Just then, a fat young man with pink cheeks broke away from the crowd and walked purposefully towards her. His expression was oddly blank. The traffic was heavy and she was unable to cross the road. As she glanced round to check his progress, she felt his hand come down heavily on the top of her head and slide back to the crown, down her neck, dragging her *hijab*.

Unfortunately for him, it was a two-piece *hijab* – an underscarf tied firmly around the head and an all-in-one overscarf that fitted the face perfectly, like that which the Somali women wear. So he only succeeded in making her forehead feel a little stretched. The traffic cleared and she took one step into the road, whispering "*Bismillah*".

Her foot landed upon a grassy hillside that was scattered with mauve-coloured crocuses. A soft, rose-scented breeze blew in her face. She was high up, overlooking a spectacular desert landscape. Sitting on a carpet, slightly higher up from where she stood, were three old men with rough white beards and tall hats. The breeze blew and the trees swayed. She could hear a waterfall nearby and again the scent of roses wafted in her face. Then she heard someone behind her shouting, voice cracking in fear.

"Oi! Oi! What's this? Stop it! What've you done?"

It was the pink-cheeked BNP protestor. The eyes of the three old men swivelled in his direction, and their smiles vanished from their faces. The BNP protestor began to run down the hill, but then stopped when he realised that there was nowhere to run to, except the desert, shimmering in the forty-five degrees heat. His cheeks grew pinker. He ran back up the hill, stumbling and panting. He decided to vent his rage on Arifa. Grimacing, he shoved his arm out and pushed her to the ground and stood over her, looking down at her with contempt. She scrambled to her feet, wondering how to deal with somebody who felt so much hatred.

One of the old men stood up and the BNP boy jumped back in panic, ready to fight, confused.

"Chubsy", said the old man, "you must control your *nafs*. You can't behave like that here. It is very ugly."

"Who you calling Chubsy? How d'you know my name is Chubsy? Who are you anyway?"

"You can call me Uncle Mudassar", said Uncle Mudassar. "We didn't invite you here, but nevertheless you *are* here, so it must be for a reason."

"I don't get it", said Chubsy. "I feel like I'm tripping. What is this place?"

'This is the *khanqah* near Qamsar, where they make rose water. You can take some back to your friends if you like; but first, why don't you sit down and have some tea? You've got too much fire burning in your head', replied Uncle Mudassar.

'Qamsar! Where's Qamsar? Sounds like some foreign place. I'm English, I am. I belong in England.'

'Qamsar is in Iran. It is famous for its gardens. Do you like gardens?'

Chubsy frowned. Did he like gardens? All his life he had only seen concrete. Of course he had been to Greenwich Park once or twice, but that was only really to target the foreigners, when they were having their music concerts.

'Well...' he shrugged, 'I've been to Greenwich Park. It was all right.'

He trod edgily from foot to foot.

'Sit down and have some tea. Then we can show you our garden.'

At that moment, Chubsy shot a distrustful glance at Arifa, which she returned with a silent, watchful glare. The other two old men also watched Chubsy warily, as he surrendered to Uncle Mudassar's invitation. Uncle Mudassar turned to Arifa.

'Sit down, little sister. You have come here too early, but I think your soul has been inclined to leave the material realm, hasn't it.'

Arifa's heart seemed to move. She sat down, wondering if she had died and was going to stay at the *khanqah* for ever.

'We wanted to take you somewhere, little sister', said Uncle Mudassar and the two other old men smiled and nodded, their eyes glowing. 'A place of knowledge, to which you might return at any time – but... with Chubsy here... I am not sure...'

'Here!', interrupted Chubsy indignantly. 'What's wrong with me? There's nothing wrong with me!'

Uncle Mudassar looked at him, puzzled, contemplating. He turned to the samovar in front of him, underneath which a short candle warmed the tea. There were also four glasses, a large bowl of sugar lumps and a plate of cream cakes. Uncle Mudassar picked up the plate and offered the cakes to Chubsy.

'What are they?' demanded Chubsy.

'Cream cakes', said Uncle Mudassar. 'Iran is famous for its cakes.'

'Yeah I know what cream cakes are! I have seen cream cakes before', Chubsy retorted defensively, irrelevantly.

Affecting a kind of nonchalance, he reached out and took one, although Arifa could see that he was not sure if he should eat it.

'Eat it', said Uncle Mudassar, and he smiled.

Without returning the smile, Chubsy put the whole cake in his mouth. Uncle Mudassar poured him some tea and placed the glass on a saucer, accompanied by two sugar lumps. He held the saucer out to Chubsy, who took it while still negotiating the cream cake, which at last he swallowed. Uncle Mudassar then poured tea for Arifa and, likewise, offered her a cream cake. After that, the two elderly gentlemen helped themselves. Uncle Mudassar sat with nothing.

'So where's your nuclear bomb?' Chubsy suddenly asked, raising a curious eyebrow.

'Excuse me?' said Uncle Mudassar.

'Your nuclear bomb. In my country they say you're going to bomb our country – that you've got a nuclear bomb, or something.'

Arifa's muscles grew tense, as she wondered how Uncle Mudassar would respond to such rudeness, but Uncle Mudassar remained tranquil.

'Chubsy, we – myself and my two fellow friends of Allah here – we do not concern ourselves with mirages. We are only interested in what is real.'

'Eh?' said Chubsy.

'You are talking about the big fantasy that is being played out in your realm, aren't you: that big fantasy of conflict that the magicians of your realm are conjuring up.'

Chubsy chuckled.

"What magicians?' he scoffed. 'I'm talking about them Muslims – in your country and in our country. They want to bomb us and kill us and destroy our culture and rule the world. It's been in the news. They say Iran wants to bomb us.'

'Yes, Chubsy, I'm sure they do, but we are only concerned with reality. We are not interested in mirages and false wars. The people in your realm who are weaving the narrative of conflict, I call them magicians, because magicians create illusions in order to gain power. It's tedious; it's draining; it's meaningless; it's a waste of time', said Uncle Mudassar.

Chubsy stared at Uncle Mudassar in silence, then wiped his mouth thoughtfully on the back of his sleeve. Arifa felt her soul grow lighter.

'Well', said Chubsy slowly, 'in our great city of London, which is overrun by your lot, they bombed us and killed loads of people. That's why we want your lot out of our country.'

'All of this, Chubsy, is the result of the great fantasy of conflict that has been spun for the last two hundred years. Your lot plundered our resources and supported a dictator who tortured us and killed us. All of this is a vortex of darkness. We have to find a way of remaining free of it. It is a drama conducted by magicians and if we don't keep a cool head, our lives will become entangled in their spell.'

Chubsy again looked thoughtful. Then he said,

'And you beat your women. You lot are wife beaters. That's why we want you out of our country.'

'So you don't attack women then?' interjected Arifa.

Chubsy looked at her coldly.

'Let's go for a walk around the garden', said Uncle Mudassar. 'There are more accurate things to talk about and to think about.'

He stood up, as did the two elderly gentlemen. Arifa drained her glass and followed them. Chubsy got up too, quickly snatching another cream cake as he did so and stuffing it into his mouth. All five of them walked up to the top of the hill, where there was a small pavilion with a balcony and behind it, a large garden filled with different varieties of rose, all emitting different scents. Straight, neatly-clipped pathways cut through the roses to the other side, where there was a hedge with an open doorway in it. Uncle Mudassar told Chubsy and Arifa about the different kinds of rose and they stopped to smell each kind, comparing the scents.

'Where d'you get all these roses?' Chubsy asked.

'They have been grown here for at least three thousand years. Sometimes travelling merchants would collect varieties from India and China and bring them back here. We can make different kinds of rose water from them, for different purposes', replied Uncle Mudassar.

'This kind', added one of the elderly gentlemen, 'is very good for soothing the brain.'

Chubsy was not sure how to take that remark and he lapsed into silence again. Arifa's soul breathed the scents and yearned to fly, only its consciousness of Chubsy kept it tethered to the ground, unable to let go. Uncle Mudassar led

them to the other side of the garden and through
the doorway. On the other side, quite to Arifa's
surprise, was a large, milky stretch of water that
continued into the distance. She could not make
up her mind whether it was a lake, or an ocean.
She could not figure out, either, how it could be
here, all the way up in the mountains. On its
horizon was what appeared to be an island.
Chubsy stood and stared. There was certainly
something compelling about the milky-white
lake. He looked troubled.

Uncle Mudassar went down to the water's
edge, where, tied to a stake, was a wooden
rowing boat and in it, two oars. Arifa followed
him, the two elderly gentlemen after her, and
Chubsy last.

"I think that there is enough room for all of
us", said Uncle Mudassar. "Chubsy and I can
row. Sister Arifa and my dear friends of Allah
can sit in the middle."

"I'm not going in that thing!' protested
Chubsy. 'You must be joking, mate!"

"Oh", said Uncle Mudassar. "All right then,
you can stay here Chubsy. We are going to that
island over there. I can't guarantee when we will
be back... but we will try to come back soon –
perhaps in about six months. I wish you well –"

"You can't just leave me like that!" cried
Chubsy. "What am I supposed to do here? Pick
roses or summink?"

"We are going to the island. If you want to come, you are welcome. If you don't, then we will see you soon... hopefully..."

"S'pose I got no choice then, have I? I can't stay here on me own, can I?" grumbled Chubsy.

"Right then", said Uncle Mudassar, and he climbed into the boat, moving carefully to the front, where he sat down and took up an oar.

Arifa then climbed in, anxious to keep as far away from Chubsy as possible. The two elderly gentlemen followed her, seated themselves in the boat and waited for Chubsy to get in. He looked nervously at the boat.

"You know I can't swim, don't you", he muttered.

"Just climb in the way you have seen us do", said Uncle Mudassar gently. "We haven't even disembarked yet."

The boat was still drawn up on the bank of the lake, one end of it on dry land.

"And as you do so", said Uncle Mudassar, "just unwind the rope and give the boat a push, so that it will slide into the water."

Chubsy breathed heavily and frowned with concentration, murmuring,

"I can't believe I'm doing this. If I ever tell anybody they're going to say Chubsy's barkin'. I'll lose all my mates."

With some effort he finally managed to give the boat a push and hurriedly climbed in, making it rock unsteadily. He gripped the sides for dear life.

"Take the oar", instructed Uncle Mudassar.

Chubsy looked about for the oar and picked it up with both hands, this time gripping on to that for dear life.

Uncle Mudassar then recited *ayat al-kursī* beautifully and asked Allah to give them a safe and beneficial journey, after which he sent salutations upon the Prophet and his family. Then he lightly placed the oar in the water and with one stroke they were gliding speedily over the milky lake, leaving the shore behind. Chubsy barely needed to row. Arifa tried to pretend that he was not there and turned her attention to the milky lake that stretched out endlessly on either side, and the receding shore, lined with the hedge of the rose garden. For her, this was a journey of which her soul had only glimpsed in dreams – the kind of dreams from which it did not want to wake. She felt at peace, as if she was finally where she really belonged.

"So where we goin'?" asked Chubsy, still looking worried.

One of the elderly gentlemen turned to him.

"To that island over there. It is a place where knowledge is transmitted to those who are worthy."

"What kind of knowledge?" asked Chubsy.

"If you are worthy, then you will find out", replied the elderly gentleman.

At the elderly gentleman's words, Arifa felt excited and nervous and wondered whether she was worthy. Then she wondered whether

Chubsy was worthy. Nobody could judge another person, or knew what was in their heart.

The boat rapidly approached the island. Arifa turned to look. She could see a number of high, white walls, inset with even higher, white towers, from which flew emerald green flags. Her heart pounded with apprehension and curiosity. Chubsy looked dubious. The elderly gentlemen were serene. Uncle Mudassar steered the boat with his oar, until it drew up alongside a landing jetty. There was a rope in the prow, which he tied around a metal ring on the jetty. Metal rings, forming a ladder, were embedded in one of its pillars. These he climbed, until he was standing on the jetty. Arifa managed to climb the ladder herself. Then Uncle Mudassar helped the two elderly gentlemen and Chubsy, who was terrified of falling into the water.

They proceeded up a grassy bank that was filled with flowers of all kinds, quivering in the soft breeze. From behind the walls, laughter echoed. Uncle Mudassar led the way to a large, arched door and knocked. It opened wide and he entered. Arifa and the others followed. The door closed behind them. Inside, they found a huge city whose houses and streets were made of glistening marble. Everybody was youthful, with shining faces, smiling, beautifully dressed and smelling of amber. Uncle Mudassar led Arifa, the two elderly gentlemen and Chubsy through the winding streets, until they could see ahead of them a high mountain, topped by a sacred building that was shaded by cypress trees. Like the banks going down to the lake, the mountain was covered with flowers of all kinds. As they approached it, the streets began to slope upwards and there were more steps to climb. Arifa was concerned about the two elderly gentlemen, but they seemed, if anything, to have more energy than both she and Chubsy, who kept stopping to gain his breath, his face now permanently marked with a troubled expression.

At last they reached the foot of the mountain, where they would have to climb a long, winding path of steep steps. A noble-looking man came towards them. He wore a green *amamah* and a long green coat over his *jubba*. Uncle Mudassar took his hand and hugged him, showing great respect for him, even though the man was his junior. He turned to Arifa and explained that the man was a close descendent of the Prophet. From now on, he would be leading them on their journey.

It was as they were about to begin the ascent of the steep steps, that they heard someone cry out behind them. They turned to see that Chubsy had decided to sit down and was refusing to move any further.

"I ain't goin' nowhere. I'm tired. My legs are aching. My head is aching", he complained. "My head is aching and ... and... I've had enough. I want to go home. I don't belong here."

He looked gloomy, staring out at the spectacular city-scape of gleaming, marble arcades, turrets and walk-ways lined with jasmine.

The man with the green *amamah* looked at Chubsy with compassion. He trod carefully down the narrow pathway, past the company, until he reached Chubsy, where he knelt down on one knee. Everybody watched coolly, but intently, at how he would handle Chubsy, but for some reason they could not exactly hear what he said, except for the words 'invited' and 'gift', although Arifa observed that it was not so much his words of reassurance, as his personality that seemed to set Chubsy at ease. He patted Chubsy on the shoulder, as if Chubsy were his brother and Chubsy got to his feet, looking almost dignified.

The *sayyid* then stepped carefully back to the front of the line and began to lead them up the mountain. Far from becoming fatigued, as Arifa had expected, through climbing such a steep slope, she began to feel stronger and more energetic than she had done in a long time. Every time the breeze blew there was a harmonious murmur of voices that was not quite human, yet which was one of the most beautiful sounds she had ever heard.

Half-way up the mountain they all had an opportunity to stop and look at the view. A balcony had been built on top of the rock face, upon which they could lean, while the *sayyid* pointed out significant landmarks. Stretching out before them was a vast plain that disappeared into a mauve haze. Interspersed throughout that plain were mountain ranges, and tucked in between the mountain ranges were other diaphanous cities of varying sizes.

"That one over there is Jabalqā. And that one is Jabarsā. My father has mentioned them."

When he said 'my father', everybody knew that he meant the noble Prophet.

"*SallAllahu alayhi wa ālih*", muttered one of the elderly gentlemen reverently.

As they continued their climb up the mountain, the laughter from the city down below floated up in small ripples. The path began to level out and they could see ahead of them the grassy summit and the sacred building surrounded by cypress trees. The building was also of marble. Nesting on its moss-covered roof were several pairs of doves.

The *sayyid* led them to the steps of the building and inside, where they found a spacious, but humble interior, the floor covered with woven carpets, a door on the other side of the room shaded by a transparent curtain, letting in only a little late afternoon light. It was quiet and peaceful and felt homely. The *sayyid* asked them to sit down in a circle, which they did. He sat down too and they waited for him to speak; but he did not speak. He simply sat and then he closed his eyes. Uncle Mudassar did the same and the two elderly gentlemen likewise. Not wanting to have to face Chubsy alone, Arifa also closed her eyes. It was then that she felt a presence in the room, as if somebody had entered. She felt it strongly in her heart. She also felt that it was somebody who she knew very well and who she loved.

Then she felt herself instantly transported to a space that consisted purely of light. It was a space that had only been briefly revealed to her when listening to a sacred recitation. Now she was there in an expanse that coloured her memories of London grey; that reduced the dimensions of that city and civilisation to utter flatness; that made the mosques only pale, poor attempts at a reflection of that which shone with an overwhelming, overpowering brightness. The sweetness and splendour of that light made her realise that this was just a taste of the knowledge of the path; that it lay concealed just behind the pages of the Holy Book; hidden behind the smiles of the learned; wrapped in the sayings of the Chosen One.

Her spirit flew, and she understood the freedom of the prophetic way. Her spirit sang and resonated with joy. She was filled with contentment and understood something of what it was to be a real human being, unencumbered by the daily dross of the material realm.

How long she was in that state, she did not know, but suddenly she found herself with her eyes open. The *sayyid* was sitting thoughtfully, as were the two elderly gentlemen. Uncle

Mudassar was just bringing a polished tin tray bearing a tall, glass jug of lemonade and a number of engraved glasses. He placed it on the floor in front of them all. Arifa looked at Chubsy. He seemed to be asleep, head drooping, eyes closed, gentle snores emanating from his nose. Uncle Mudassar poured lemonade for the *sayyid*, for Arifa and the two elderly gentlemen. The *sayyid* held the glass of lemonade in front of him, looked at it as if it was a miracle and whispered *"Bismillah al-Rahman al-Rahim"*, whereupon Chubsy let out a loud snore, opened his eyes, and in some confusion uttered the word "Mum". Realising what he had just said and the company he was in, he blushed and tried to adopt the stony look he was accustomed to wearing on the street. Arifa tried not to smirk. She found it, actually, rather touching.

After they had drunk their lemonade, the *sayyid* led them back down the mountain. They all walked in silence, still attached to the space of light in which they had flown. Arifa wondered whether Chubsy had experienced it too. She thought she detected a difference in him, although she was not sure.

When they reached the bottom of the mountain, the *sayyid* wished them farewell and a safe journey. Uncle Mudassar took his hand and thanked him. The two elderly gentlemen bowed their heads respectfully, beaming, their faces glowing. The *sayyid* gave a nod to Arifa and said lightly, but not without significance, "We are always here." Too shy to say anything else, she answered simply, "Thank you." The *sayyid* turned to Chubsy, who blinked at him in return, frowning slightly.

"I hope you have enjoyed your journey", said the *sayyid*.

"Yeah... nice one, mate. Cheers. 'Preciate it", answered Chubsy, as if the *sayyid* was his brother, although his tone was solemn.

After that, Uncle Mudassar led them back through the city. Arifa began to feel a kind of pain in her body. She realised she did not want to leave. Why should she, when she had found a place where she belonged? She anticipated her return with dread. She knew she was going back to the material realm.

The boat journey across the milk-white lake seemed to pass in a blur and before she knew it, they had disembarked on the other side and were approaching the doorway to the rose garden. Misgivings piled up inside her mind, one upon the other. She looked at all the varieties of rose, with their different scents, and felt heart-broken at having to leave them. There in front of them was the pavilion, then the view of the gardens at the foot of the hill, then the desert, still shimmering in the reddish evening heat. On the hillside, purple with a sea of crocuses, was the carpet on which they had sat, the plate with a few cream cakes, the empty tea glasses. Shadows were lengthening across the grass. She couldn't bear it.   Desperate, she appealed to Uncle Mudassar.

"I don't want to go! I don't want to go back!"

All of them turned to her, surprised by her sudden outburst. For some reason, Chubsy hung his head.

"Little sister, you have been given a taste of the knowledge now", replied Uncle Mudassar. "It is for you to keep. And don't forget what the *sayyid* said – "

A motorbike roared past her. Then a bus. Diesel fumes filled her nostrils. She could hear the baying of men's voices. She turned. The demonstration. East London mosque. Then she realised that, standing behind her, was Chubsy. He looked at her, but his expression revealed nothing. Instinctively, she went to cross the road. She ran. Reaching the other side, she glanced back again. There was Chubsy, still standing, still facing her, looking oddly passive, his arms by his side. Then he put his hand to his head and looked down, either thinking, reflecting or confused.

She hurried down the road, past the East London mosque, further on still. She glanced back. There was Chubsy, standing motionless, his hand to his head. Up ahead, on her left, she noticed two old men sitting on a bench. One had a walking stick. Two old men, come to watch the demonstration probably. She sped past them. The words "Wait, little sister" reached her ears above the roar of the traffic. She stopped, turned and recognised them. They both smiled and nodded. One of them raised his hand and held out a rose.

Atsumori

This story continues the great tradition which began in Japan in the twelfth century, of telling about a series of particular events, whose hero was named Atsumori. It haunts me to this day, as it has haunted generations. But I will leave it to Renshō to tell, as he was there when it happened.

If you awaken from the dream that is this world, you will know what is real... Ah, you are wondering who I am and why I carry this rosary in my hand. I am, in fact, the one who killed Atsumori. He was the same age as my own son, but I had to kill him, as our two clans were at war.

Before I became a monk, I was one of the best soldiers of the Minamoto clan. Then, my name was Kumagai. I was from the province of Musashi, to the east of Miyako, the splendid capital city of my country, today known as Kyoto. Atsumori was of the Heike, who ruled in Miyako. They were wealthy and of course very cultured. They practiced poetry and commissioned great works of art. They built palaces and temples, and expanded the borders of the city. The mansions of their aristocrats lined the streets. But they did not know how much they were hated. Yes, they were hated, because they were proud; they were arrogant, oppressing the farmers and craftsmen, demanding impossible taxes, ignoring the distant villages that suffered in times of a bad harvest. They thought about nobody except themselves.

We had the backing of the people when we decided to attack. Our army was well organised. We all thought as one. I only cared about my mission, fulfilling my orders, and of the triumph that would follow. We knew we were going to win. The Heike had been warned of our attack, as a courtesy, so that the women and children could leave Miyako first, but they did not take us seriously, for some reason. Perhaps because of their intoxication with power, or perhaps they thought we were just a barbaric people from the east and that they would easily be able to fend us off.

We set out at night towards Miyako and reached its peaked roofs before dawn, just when the temple bells were beginning to chime. Then our army flooded into the city. Those who were beginning to set up their stalls cowered away in fear. People began to panic. I remember how they ran into their homes. Others got down on their knees and bowed their heads, begging for mercy, just in case one of our army might feel like cutting somebody's head off; but we were disciplined: we headed straight for the palace quarters. It was then that the soldiers of the Heike appeared. They had been positioned in a circle around the palace grounds: the archers, then the foot soldiers, then the cavalry. At last we had the battle we had been waiting for, but they were outnumbered and their will was weak. We had been told by our general to have no mercy and we followed his orders, decimating them in a matter of hours.

We never knew the sacred law
And thought we would live forever
We did not know that all greatness vanishes
As swiftly as the spark of a flint

It is strange to think how I felt then: my emotions were cool; I was filled with determination; I feared nothing – certainly not death. It was when I saw Atsumori's flute that everything changed. After that, I cried and cried – but we will come to that shortly.

I remember how the sun gradually rose over the city with long, slow beams of light. I remember the sound of the cockerels crowing and babies crying. A lot of people decided to flee. We saw them hurrying away, a few belongings packed on hand-drawn carts, bumping and crashing through the streets – many headed north. As soon as the Heike clan had realised that they were beaten, they fled westwards, before our army could reach them. We arrived at their palace quarters to find them empty, except for the servants, who were taken prisoner. I remember how some of them protested and lamented.

Half of our army remained at the palace, while the other half headed out of the city, westwards in the direction of Suma bay, that beautiful stretch of seaside where the saltmakers worked all day. It was autumn, and flocks of plovers were flying overhead. The salty breeze blew in, tinged with ice.

> *At Suma bay there grows no bamboo*
> *For flutes such as Little Branch;*
> *You may only find a wooden flute*
> *Left from our saltmaker's fires*

Our army arrived at the sandy beach to find the Heike loading their ships, ready to set sail, though who knows where they were thinking of going. The ships looked oddly fragile, bouncing on the rough waves. They had taken the emperor with them. His name was Antoku. He was still only a child, hardly fit to rule yet, but descended from the great line that went back one thousand years.

Our army assembled quickly, so that we were able to look down on to the shore as the Heike set sail. That morning the wind was in their favour and their ships made fast progress. Only a few aristocrats and some of the Heike army remained on the beach. Our general told us to finish them off. We charged forward, filling the air with our war cries, our swords held out in front of us, one hand on the reins. We saw those who were left on the beach scatter in different directions – all except for one man. To my astonishment he was galloping back towards us. He stopped on the sand and like lightning dismounted, reaching down, picking something up and placing it in a brocade bag that was tied to his waist. Then he mounted again and as fast as he possibly could, he galloped back to the sea.

It was not long before I caught up with him. He was trying to swim his horse towards the ships, but they were already too far out, although I could hear some faint cries, as some of his friends on the decks tried to encourage him to hurry. I charged into the water and swam my horse towards his, raising my war fan to challenge him to a fight. He struggled to turn his horse around in order to face me and took his sword out of its scabbard. Our blades clashed several times until we both fell from our horses into the sea, where we continued to fight, but he was small and light and no match for me. I ripped off his war helmet, ready to cut off his head. There before me was a boy no older than my own son. He was probably only about fourteen or fifteen. He did not look defiant, just ready for his fate. He knew he was going to die.

This was the first time in my career as a soldier that I had not wanted to kill the enemy. There had been opportunities before when I could have shown mercy, but we were always commanded to complete the job, and I had always executed my enemy without a moment's hesitation. This time, I observed in myself a great weakness. Was it because I was getting old? It was surely a sign that I was no longer fit to be a part of the army. I was loath to see this boy dead, although there was little that I could do.

"You know, don't you, that if I let you go, there is a crowd of soldiers behind me who will kill you without a moment's thought? At least if I execute you I can promise to pray for the peace of your soul."

He did not say a word. Instead, he lifted back his head, exposing his throat. I did the job, as easily as cutting a piece of silk in half. His horse had already swum for the shore and was taken by one of our men. Carrying Atsumori's head in one hand, I dragged his body to the beach, and laid it out in the sand, the waves lapping at his feet. Then I caught sight of the brocade bag tied around his waist. I opened it, to find a smooth, polished bamboo flute with a tassel tied around its neck. On the back, burnt into the reed stem, were two characters, spelling out the name 'Little Branch'.

Our generation dissolved like a dream
We were like leaves stripped from the trees
Scattered in the winds
Lost to the four directions

Tears seeped from behind the mask of my war helmet. I knelt beside Atsumori's body like somebody utterly helpless. I felt as if I was a dying star tumbling through the cosmos. The sand seemed to slip away from beneath me. The waves deafened me and the cries of the Heike and Minamoto sounded like that of seagulls, vanishing into the clouds. Several of my fellow soldiers galloped over to me.

"Hey! Kumagai! What are you doing? Everything is over! We've won! Come on! Let's get back to the city!"

I got to my feet, clutching Atsumori's flute.

"Hey! Kumagai! What's wrong with you? Come on! Let's get back to the city!"

***

Minamoto no Yoshinaka did not want to accept my resignation. It was a difficult moment. He talked to me at length, offering me time to think about my decision. I was one of his best soldiers. I had to insist that I was not going to change my mind. And so, he let me go.

I walked through the city that we had conquered, yet I saw that even our time would eventually come. I could not escape from the thought that everything must end, fearful that, while we celebrated our triumph, we were only living in an illusion. And I still felt Atsumori's death on my hands.

Returning to the vacated mansion that was once inhabited by one of the Heike aristocrats and now allocated to me for my family, I announced to my wife and children that I was renouncing the world. This did not mean that I was leaving them, as many who take the path do, but that I would now be occupied with prayers and contemplation.

I joined a local order and took a new name, Renshō. I was ordained into certain sacred practices, a plain and rigorous way of life, with little sleep and simple food; but, as you know, this was not just to save myself. I felt Atsumori close to me all the time and I had to fulfil the promise that I had made him. My days were spent in praying for the peace of his soul.

About a year after our conquest of Miyako, I went once again down to Suma bay, to reflect upon the battle that had taken place there. The remaining Heike had gone into exile – we do not know where exactly – perhaps to China or Korea. The skies were overcast and there on the beach, as always, were the saltmaker's fires, greenish plumes of smoke rising into the air. The beach was as quiet as if no battle had ever taken place. The sand was smooth. The hoof prints of our horses had long since faded.

From a distance I could hear the singing of a group of saltmakers, who were gathered around a fire. I could see that they were young boys of varying ages. Their song was a little sad, as many of our folksongs are. They sang of loneliness and I felt the meaning of their words. I decided to go and greet them and to listen to them more closely, for I was certain that I had heard one of them playing a flute, something which only priests or aristocrats were meant to do.

"Excuse me. Was one of you playing a flute just now?"

They looked up at me all at once and one of them answered cautiously,

"Yes, it was one of us."

"That is a very refined thing for you to do", I said, then immediately regretted my words.

"'A very refined thing for us to do?' Haven't you heard the saying 'Envy none above you, despise none below you'? Our songs have inspired court poets for centuries. And think of all the famous flutes which have played our tunes: Little Branch, Cicada Wing and Greenleaf, to name but a few."

I felt shame: I, who was trying to practice a path of humility, had expressed such a class-ridden blunder; and I, now a monk, was the one who owned Little Branch, because of what I had done...

"You are right", I answered. "Please forgive me."

They continued their song until the end, then each got up and went together with their buckets, down to the shore, bidding me farewell, except for one young boy who remained, and who I was certain I had seen before.

"I see you are staying here alone", I remarked. "Why is that?"

"Because I have been called here. I left this world in a state of conflict, and still I can't rest, but I heard somebody calling the Name for me and so I came, as it gives me comfort."

He had the same clear expression as he who I now prayed for daily, and yet he looked a little different – but who else could it be? I did not dare to think it. Yet in spite of myself I said, "Atsumori" and at exactly that moment he said, "Atsumori, my name is Atsumori."

He looked at me.

"It is you – "

"It is I who am praying for you."

"If you can release me from my sorrow through the comfort of your prayer – "

"If you can release me from my guilt – "

"And I can find welcome – "

"In the One who abandons no one."

That was the day that I saw Atsumori. I have not seen him since. Perhaps he has gone at last, in peace. I am still waiting…

The Ink of the Scholar

Since his retirement from teaching, Ibrahim had taken to studying the great figures of Islamic history and to writing about them in a way that might be easy for his grandchildren to understand. This task had become all-absorbing and only the sound of the *adhān* took his attention away from his work. The *adhān* emanated from the sanctified precincts of Sayyeda Zaynab's shrine and resonated through the streets, almost stirring the dust, penetrating the thin walls of Ibrahim's apartment, and he noticed, too, that the birds were always silent at that time.

Since he had retired, he had been able to concentrate on prayer. His son deposited a little salary into his bank account, which he was able to live on if he was careful. These days the world had ceased to mean very much to him, and even if some rude young boys might bump into him in the street, or someone might impatiently beep their horn at him when he was crossing the road, none of it seemed to matter; and soon he would be gone, and soon he would be forgotten.

He had noticed, too, that there was often a brilliant light in front of his eyes, when his forehead was pressed to the ground in *sujūd*. He did not tell anybody about this, for fear of sounding as if he was bragging. Then sometimes when he entered the shrine of Sayyeda Zaynab, with its crystal-like ceiling of fractured mirrors that echoed with the sobbing of women, he would sit quietly in a corner, contemplating, and a tremendous power would enter him, which melted his heart utterly and he would press his hand to his forehead as tears soaked into his cotton shirt.

What was to happen next to Ibrahim, however, he was unable to keep to himself. It was one morning, after *fajr*, as the sky was turning blue and the air was growing hot, and he sat at his wooden desk, head bent closely over the page, stacks of history books and papers piled up around him, that he arrived at the moment where Sayyedna 'Ali was about to be martyred. It was a terrible thing to write about. He felt his whole being gripped with apprehension. He wanted to put it in simple language. It was important to make it clear and easy to understand. Ibn Muljam, the assassin, was sitting amongst the men as Sayyedna 'Ali came out to lead the *fajr* prayer. In an instant, before anyone knew what was happening, Ibn Muljam had leapt to his feet, at the same time raising his sword high above his head. He brought it with full force down upon Sayyedna Ali's skull and blood gushed down Sayyedna 'Ali's face.

And blood gushed down Sayyedna 'Ali's face... As Ibrahim wrote these words his pen appeared to leak suddenly. A pool of ink poured from the nib and smeared across the page. Then he realised that it was not ink, but blood, for it was red. He cried out, threw down the pen and flew back from the desk so quickly that he knocked his chair flying.

Without any further thought he rushed to the living room, picked up the phone and dialled his son's number. His son was just about to leave for work.

"Ahmed!" Ibrahim cried. "Come quickly! Something's happened!"

"Baba what is it? Are you all right?"

There could be no denying that the substance smeared across the page was blood. When Ahmed saw it, his whole body went cold and he shivered violently.

"Ahmed", whispered Ibrahim with eyes wide, "what does this mean, do you think?"

But Ahmed could not reply, for at the sight of the blood, the full impact of Sayyedna 'Ali's assassination hit him as it had never done before in his life and he hurried from the room, choking.

News of the incident spread quickly throughout the neighbourhood and Ibrahim found that there was a constant knocking on his door by those who wanted to see what had happened. He let people in to look at the sight of the pen left abandoned, the pool of blood, still strangely red, smeared across the page, and it had the same effect upon them as it had done Ahmed. It was as if they were experiencing the event of Sayyedna 'Ali's assassination for the first time, and they left, covering their eyes with the ends of their scarves or their hands, crying as if their hearts had broken. There were others, however, who came and looked at Ibrahim strangely. They did not return his greeting, and once, one of them whispered to him: "You will pay for your lies."

Upon these words, he reflected, a few days later, that he must put the pen and page in safe keeping with Sidi Abu Zayn, the imam of Sayyeda Zaynab's shrine. And as he was reflecting, he heard somebody knocking on his door. He opened it to find two men with kind, smiling faces. They said that they had heard about the extraordinary event and humbly asked if they might come to see the pen and the blood on the page for themselves. Ibrahim welcomed them warmly and invited them in, leading them upstairs to his simple study, which was filled with morning sunshine.

"Here, my brothers, you can see for yourselves. Sayyedna Ali's blood..."

Those were the last words that Ibrahim uttered, for, in a flash, one of the men pulled a knife from his sleeve. Ibrahim felt as if his body was filled with a burning light. He saw the face of his assassin: eyes like black ice, mouth pulled in a grimace filled with hatred. As he lost consciousness, he felt himself enveloped in somebody's arms and he was carried away to an ocean, where he heard the gentle recitation of the Qur'ān: *'wa illallah il-masīr'*: 'and to God is the return'.

The Beauty of the Banlieue

My friend Razia was from Mauritius. She was petite, about five feet two, slender, with large, dark eyes and a wide smile. We had met in London at a *majlis*, shortly before she moved to Toulouse to set up home with her French Muslim husband, Jacques. Toulouse is a quintessentially French city: it is clean and tidy; there are red brick pavements, museums, a town hall with its square, shops selling sweets, soaps and creams made from violets. People are smartly dressed and well-behaved. The only feature that slightly detracts from this is the ubiquitous presence of dog excrement, which decorates pavements and roads like a kind of modern art installation.

I went to visit Razia one cold weekend in early spring, in the month of *dhu'l-hijja*. She lived in a charming suburb of the city, which had neatly laid-out streets, empty of traffic, well-tended gardens and a new estate of smartly-built flats, one of which was occupied by Razia and Jacques. She was an excellent host, scrupulous about the quality of food that she cooked, immaculately tidy and when we went out shopping, she made witty observations about the city. "Let's pretend that each dog poo is a rose bud. Oops, watch out! There's another rose bud." But Razia was also lonely and missed her family in Mauritius.

Soon it would be Eid al-Adha. At home, her mother would cook a special biryani. They would put on their best clothes and go to the mosque for morning prayers. Here, in this suburb of Toulouse, everything was quiet, and, it being February, a little colourless. We decided to go and find the Muslim area, to see if there might be a mosque that we could go to on Eid; but when we went out we did not see many Muslims and even the 'Algerian quarter' consisted of just a few streets where North African goods were sold. We went into the shops to ask if they could tell us where there was a mosque, but we did not understand the directions they gave, especially the ones given in Algerian Arabic.

Razia then asked Jacques if anybody at his work would know of where there might be a mosque. Jacques returned with the answer. It was on the edge of town, but the area was dangerous and it was advisable for us not go – but our hearts yearned. We asked what time the Eid prayers were. Jacques said eight o'clock.

The next morning, Razia and I remained awake after *fajr* and prepared to go out. We had to get a bus to the centre of town and then a train, which would take us all the way north, to the very end of the line, almost out of the city. When we arrived at the other end of the line, it dawned on me what Jacques's colleague had meant by the words 'dangerous area'. It was really another way of saying 'Muslim area'.

Razia and I stepped out of the humble, concrete entrance to the station and looked around us, wondering which direction to take, for stretching in front of us were a number of poorly tarmacked roads, and then, towering on the near horizon were several vast, concrete edifices, patterned with hundreds of oblong windows. This was the *banlieue*, the ghetto, where thousands of people lived, floor upon floor upon floor.

A man passed us and walked on ahead, down a pathway that cut between these monstrous constructions. We asked him the way to the *masjid* and he indicated that he was going there himself, so we followed in his direction. We passed more edifices, towering above us on either side, to the left and to the right. In some of the windows there were house plants, in others, washing hung out to dry. The air was cool, silent.

Then, out of this grey, Cubist painting floated one or two white, shimmering shapes: women in their Eid clothes – white, glistening *jalabia*s and white or pale coloured scarves with shining pearl-like beads, or embroidered flowers. We followed them as they led a winding route, through a passageway under one of the apartment blocks and down another narrow road, towards the outskirts of the outskirts. The further we walked, the more people came floating out of the concrete – men, too, in white, wearing *amamah*s.

An atmosphere of sweet peace permeated the air. We turned a corner, and there was the mosque, which was actually an empty school building. The gateway was humming with men, women and children, everyone in their best clothes. Razia and I went through, down some steps and were instructed to enter a particular door. As we turned to enter my heart seemed to move within me, for there, row upon row, were men and women, standing or sitting, in preparation for the prayers. They were North African, Indian, West African, all in bright colours, while the air resonated with something fine, which cannot easily be described, but which is always present where there is *dhikrullah*.

Razia and I took off our shoes and carried them through the rows of people. There was no space for us inside the school building. We passed through, out to the other side, where there was a plot of land laid out with mats, and more men and women were preparing for the prayer under the pale sun. Razia and I found a place at the back, next to some Algerian women in long, cotton *hijab*s. We all greeted each other. Razia and I placed our shoes behind us on the grass and sat waiting for the Eid prayer. People were still assembling: African men in *boubou*s; young Algerian men in jeans and jackets; children of all ages. To our right, behind a row of trees, towered one of the concrete edifices, its dark windows overlooking the gathering of lights and colours.

The cool, early morning sun whispered through the bare branches of the trees and then came the Eid prayer, through loudspeakers, splitting the material realm with the words *"Allahu Akbar"*. Everybody resonated with the words, all of us dissolving into a single soul. After the first *"Allahu Akbar"* there was silence for a moment. One or two late-comers hurried to find a place. Then came the next *"Allahu Akbar"*. People stood, heads bowed, in silence. A single voice spiralled across our heads, making the air waver with the words of the Qur'ān. Then came the *ruku'* and then the *sujūd*.

After the prayer, Razia and I shook hands with the women next to us and wished for each other that our prayer be accepted. The people gathered together in groups and slowly trickled through the mosque, out into the road, where they stood exchanging news, talking in low tones, laughing, while the children played together. Razia and I walked with contentment. We had entered another space where the spirit could expand and breathe. We took the route back through the ghetto blocks, along the flat, concrete pathways, past the concrete playground to the station, with its plain, square, concrete entrance.

Back in the centre of town, we headed towards the 'Algerian quarter' and found a café down a side-street that sold traditional sweets and coffee. There we had our Eid breakfast, the only customers at that time of the day. Razia talked about the biryani she was going to make, the same as her mother's back in Mauritius. Then it would be an almost perfect Eid.

We went to the bus stop to head home, past the shop that sold violet-flavoured sweets, through the square with the old town hall and past the museum. As we waited for our bus, clinging to the beauty of our Eid morning, Razia suddenly said,

"I think that woman likes my face. She keeps looking at me."

Standing near us was a middle-aged woman, wearing a smart coat and carrying a large, black handbag. She seemed to be looking at Razia in alarm, although when I turned to her, she quickly looked away. It was a mystery as to why she was so nervous.

Our bus arrived, which happened to be the one for which the woman was waiting. She boarded first. We got on after her and sat down. She stood opposite us, staring at us. We decided to ignore her, and talked between ourselves. The bus wound its way out of town to the neatly-clipped suburbs and all the time the woman clutched her handbag as she kept a watchful eye on us. We were aliens in an alien world.

The bus drew up to an isolated bus stop and Razia said, "This is ours." We stood up. At the same time, the woman moved towards the door, so that Razia and I were obliged to stand behind her. Only the three of us got off. Of course, this must have been the woman's worst nightmare: two thieves, or terrorists, following her to an isolated bus stop so that they could snatch her handbag. She clutched it tightly and shot off down the road, not quite running, turning a corner, out of sight. It just so happened to be the corner that we needed to turn, although by the time that we had reached there, she had long since disappeared – perhaps she was hiding behind a bush somewhere. I wondered what story she would tell her friends and family.

New Civilisation

Once upon a time there was a beautiful valley set between some mountains. It was an ancient valley which had been inhabited for thousands of years. During most months, the sun shone across its green, abundant fields, which were filled with violets. A fresh breeze blew from the snowcapped mountains, so that the scent of the violets wafted across the roofs of the houses, which were inlaid with precious stones. Goat herders spent the summer high up near the mountain peaks, passing their nights in specially built wooden shelters. Women sat outside their doorsteps together, combing out the wool collected from the sheep. Men went mining in the mountains for metals and minerals. These were then bound up on horse-drawn carts and taken to the local market, far far away, to be traded for goods such as art work, embroidered silks, scented soap and books. Few outsiders ever came to the valley, because it lay across mountainous terrain, and high, perilous paths had to be crossed in order to reach it. And so, when the twentieth century came and went, and the twenty-first century arrived, the valley was still the same as it had been for hundreds of years, except that now could heard the low hum of generators producing electricity for refrigerators and lamps.

Since he was a little boy, Mark's one ambition had been to become a trader: to pack up the minerals and metals from the mines, and take the long journey over the mountains to the market where he would sell his goods, and come back with surprises for everyone in the valley. People always came running out of their houses when the traders came back, entering the valley like heroes, with beautiful things from another world. When he reached the age of sixteen, close to marriageable age, another ambition grew in his heart: to marry the daughter of his father's best friend. Her name was Sophia. She was fourteen and a half, and she could spent hours at a loom, carefully weaving cloth, which would be used for everything from carpets, to shirts, to gloves which fitted perfectly whoever needed them. Whenever one of the traders came back to the valley, she would be the first to jump up to see what they had brought, and always seemed to love the beautiful things more than anyone else, a love which seemed to arise out of a fascination for the places from which they came.

So Mark had decided that she was the girl who would be perfect as his wife. He could be a trader and then come back to the valley, his cart loaded with wondrous gifts, and Sophia would jump up and run to greet him and admire all the things which he had brought.

The people in the valley could trace their genealogies back more than a thousand years, and winter nights were spent gathered around fires, as the elders told stories of their ancestors, of their exploits and discoveries, and of their loyalty to the valley, the place to which they would always return. It was a matter of pride for the community that their roots lay in the valley; that they belonged there and that they had such an ancient history.

* * *

One spring morning, Mark was awoken by a noise which he had never heard before in his life: the sound of somebody screaming. He sat up in bed, then rushed to the window and looked down into the street below. His parents were already there, along with several neighbours who were trying to calm the screaming person. It was one of the goat herd boys. He had run all the way down from the top of the mountain without stopping, losing one of his shoes on the way. He was so hysterical that he could hardly speak, but finally he managed to get some words out. He had been sleeping in his wooden shelter, woken up to the cock crow to begin a day's work, stepped outside to stretch his arms and get some fresh air, when he found that half of his flock lay dead, while the other half had been gathered into a corner of the field where they grazed, penned in by metal shields. Standing around the shields, forming a human wall, was an army of strange-looking men with large helmets and big black sunglasses. They all had weapons slung over their shoulders and wore large boots.

Instinctively, the goat herd boy ran away as fast as he could, and it was then that shots were fired and bullets bounced off the ground just behind him. As he ran across the field, he caught sight of more strange-looking men, all wearing helmets and big black sunglasses, marching in lines, weapons at the ready, along one of the narrow winding paths that led down into the valley. He hid behind some bushes until they were gone, and took a short cut down the mountain, but whichever route he took there were groups of these men, either standing in the form of human barricades, setting up camp, or slaughtering whatever animal they could find.

At last he managed to find the main road down into the valley, but noticed as he went that on almost every mountainside, the strange men had set up camp and were building walls on which they placed their weapons. The whole valley was surrounded.

This was his story, and after him came other goat herders, all running headlong into the village in a state of fear and panic, and all announcing the same.

* * *

Friday 24th May

I travelled with the Allies to a valley which I have been told is an outpost of resistance against the liberation. Their job is to pacify any potential rebellion, confiscate all weaponry and secure the mines, which are said to be sources of rare metals and precious stones. It is said that the people in this valley are particularly ruthless and have never entered the modern world. They live according to a fairly primitive tribal system. As a reporter, I was warned not to approach any of them, and to remain close to the army.

We entered the territory over night and were met with no resistance, but when morning came, the Allies found themselves engaged in heavy fighting with large groups of well-armed goat herders. Unfortunately some goats were killed in the process, but the Allies did all they could to protect the animals. The Allies routed the goat herders and quickly managed to surround the valley. We are now observing the village which lies down below and watching for any signs of movement.

* * *

The elders of the village called an emergency meeting in the village square. The younger generations also attended, listening intently to what should be done. The valley had never been attacked before and so there had never been any reason to build up an armoury of weapons. They had traps which they used to bait rabbits, slingshots that were used for hunting birds and some polished wooden spears, which the most skilled huntsmen of the community could use for deer. There were also pitchforks and spades, pick axes used for hacking away at the rock face under the mountains, and piles of rubble at the entrances of the mines, which might be broken into rocks and thrown if necessary.

Mark listened along with his friends. Most of all, he wondered why those strange men in helmets and dark glasses had appeared. What did they want? Would they go away if somebody spoke to them? And could they perhaps pay something in compensation for all the goats they had killed?

People in the crowd spoke up and asked just those questions to the elders, who replied, "We don't know, any more than you do, what they are doing here."

It was decided that a delegation would be sent in order to find out, and also in order to ask the strangers to leave. One member of the elders volunteered to go, and he selected two men and two women, who were the main leaders in the community. They did not know if they should go armed or not. Jeremiah, the elder, decided that he would take a pitchfork. The others were going to take pick axes, but leave them somewhere nearby, out of sight, on their way up to meeting the strangers.

At eleven o'clock, the delegation set out, with the whole community following behind them to the edge of the village, watching with silent anxiety as they headed off up the road, back towards the mountains, where indeed, even from down below there could be seen men in large, sandy-coloured outfits moving about. Jeremiah and the accompanying delegation climbed a steep, narrow path that cut through whispering grasses, where the rattle of crickets' wings eddied in the breeze and small blue butterflies danced amid the buttercups.

As everybody in the village stood waiting, staring at the point at which Jeremiah and the delegation had disappeared around a corner, they heard a short cacophony of explosions, which they later realised was gunfire. They waited until nightfall for the delegation to return, then, disheartened, retired to their homes for the night.

* * *

Saturday 25th May

As we waited for signs of movement in the village, one of the Allies caught sight of a mob armed with machetes and rifles heading out towards us. They were yelling and shouting and sounded as if they were on the warpath. They headed straight for our encampment, firing round after round, wounding three soldiers. The Allies fired back and managed to kill several dozen of

66

the rebels, while the others fled back to the village, no doubt in order to build up reinforcements and to send for more weapons.

* * *

When Jeremiah and the rest of the delegation had still not appeared by the next morning, most of the community instinctively knew that they had been killed, and a heavy weight of grief descended upon them all. The elders called another meeting, amid which there could be heard the sound of weeping. The husbands and wives of the delegation stood gravely by, their faces immobile, eyes downcast. Nana, Jeremiah's wife of some sixty years, sat rocking back and forth, sobbing into one of her homemade lace kerchiefs. The community had never encountered such ruthlessness before. Everybody was shocked and afraid. Nobody knew what to do.

Mark listened, along with the rest of the young men, and he was filled with a horrible feeling of helplessness, something which he had never felt before. He turned to his father, a hardworking miner, and a sense of despair crept into his heart when he saw the very same helplessness on the man's face. He saw the same expression on the face of his father's best friend, and he saw the fear and confusion in Sophia's eyes, as she looked this way and that at everybody gathered there, wondering what they were going to do; and then he felt a bitter, crushing sense of shame.

"Somebody has to go to retrieve the bodies", said one of the elders.

And Mark's hand shot up, as he shouted,
"I will!"

Two of his friends, Peter and Jack, also volunteered. At first there were murmurings that they were too young and the job too dangerous. A dispute broke out, which fanned into an argument. The community did not want to see their young men killed, but Mark could not bear to do nothing, and after he, Peter and Jack refused to back down, the community finally assented.

They would have to wait until nightfall, and then slip quietly up the mountain path in order to find the bodies. They were given ropes and sacks with which they could drag the bodies back to the village, where some of the miners would be waiting to take them so that they could be given a proper burial.

Such a plan proved futile, however, for that very afternoon their village was invaded by the men in sandy-coloured uniforms. First, they had blocked the entrances of the mines as they advanced upon the village, so that any miner that surfaced could immediately be apprehended; then, they surrounded the village, moving in resolutely, weapons pointed straight ahead.

It was the time of the afternoon when people usually had a siesta, just after having lunch.

Families sat in the kitchen drinking coffee, or in the shade of the eaves of their houses, as the local cats draped themselves over the front steps and chickens clucked quietly in their coops, scratching mindlessly at the straw. Of course, this siesta was not one entirely of ease; fretful conversations passed back and forth about what people thought might happen and whether they should fight or appease the invaders; and it was in the middle of these conversations that the armed men burst in, shouting in a language which nobody understood, overturning kitchen tables, upsetting pots of boiling coffee and firing at the chickens.

The whole village was filled with the sound of screams, the yelling of the men as they tried to resist, and the barking of guard dogs, which were quickly shot in order to be silenced.

The soldiers dragged everybody out of their homes: men, women, children and babies. Anyone who tried to run away was quickly caught and dragged back. They were all forced to gather in the village square, where a general stood on a chair and addressed them all, again in a language which they did not understand. He seemed to be trying to reason with them; then he asked them some questions, which he repeated again with increasing frustration and on obtaining no answers, he gave orders to his soldiers, whereupon they began to divide up the men and the women. The screaming and yelling rose to a pitch of pure panic. One of the soldiers fired shots in the air. The women were herded together and driven towards the village hall; the men into a stable where the horses were kept.

Amidst all the chaos, Mark tried to keep his eye on Sophia. She kept disappearing into the crowd. Then as the soldiers began to drive the women away, pulling them by the arms, or shoving them with the butts of their machine guns, he caught sight of a soldier reaching out and touching her cheek. She flicked his hand away as she might do a fly. He grabbed her wrist and twisted her arm back, leering over her.

"Don't touch my daughter!" her father yelled, but he was struck in the face with the butt of a machine gun and a gash appeared on his forehead.

* * *

Sunday 26th May

After the attack on the Allies, it was decided to storm the village. The army moved in, quickly and efficiently. Some soldiers were sent to guard the mines; others went ahead in the face of heavy gunfire. The rebels used women and children as human shields, which made it difficult for the Allies to approach at first, but eventually they overwhelmed the small numbers, forced them to hand over their weapons, and gathered them in the village square, where they handed out sweets as a way of conveying their friendship. General

Devere assured them that if they did not resist, then they would be treated fairly. He explained that the Allies were here to bring them a good life. If they obeyed orders, then they too could join the twenty-first century.

* * *

By evening, the men had still not been given anything to eat or drink. Probably the case was the same for the women. Fatigued, hungry and angry, Mark sat with Peter and Jack and among themselves they planned to escape from the stable, head through the mountains and get help from whomsoever they might find. If the invaders did not plan to feed anyone, then they only had a short time in which to act. The thought of leaving the village was daunting. Mark had absolutely no idea what lay beyond the mountains, or which direction he should take. It was decided to recruit one of the traders, who at least knew the roads to the next town. Samuel, a father of five children, agreed to go with them. The elders also agreed to the plan, although Mark could see from their faces that their minds were filled with doubts as to whether he could carry out the task, something which irritated him, and made him all the more determined to go ahead.

Outside the stable, a group of soldiers sat on chairs which had been taken from one of the villagers' houses, talking and smoking. Their guns were slung across their backs. There was no way that Mark and his friends could escape through that route. The only other way out was through one of the small windows that were situated high up near the roof of the stable. They were fortunate that it was a dark night. The new moon had not yet appeared. Only the stars provided light. With the help of some of the men from the village, Mark and his friends began to pile up hay under the window, in order to make a mound that might enable them to get closer to it, but even after some considerable time, the mound was not high enough as the hay became compressed. At last some of the men volunteered to form a human ladder, with three kneeling on the ground, two standing on their shoulders, and one more standing on their shoulders, so that, as they clung to the wall of the stable, Mark was able to climb up and reach the window. With all his might, he pulled himself up and squeezed through, dropping down on the other side, trying to roll as he landed, so as to break his fall.

Peter, Jack and Samuel followed, with varying degrees of difficulty. At the back of the stable was a field. At the end of the field was a winding stream, with a narrow plank that was used as a bridge. The field faced away from the village, where the soldiers were concentrating their attentions. Even so, no one could be certain where they would come across more soldiers.

They crept across the bridge and into the field on the other side, turning back briefly towards the village, to make sure that nobody had noticed them. They could still hear some of the women shouting at the soldiers; and the sound of houses being ransacked. Then they crossed the field and stealthily climbed through the trees that covered the mountainside, scarcely daring to breathe for fear of making a noise.

They trekked across the mountains until they saw the first fine line of light appearing in the darkness of the eastern sky. They stopped to pray and to concentrate their minds. There were still soldiers camped out on the mountainsides. Coming back would be another fraught journey. Eventually they found the main road that led to the next town, the one that Samuel always took; but they preferred to follow it by walking amidst the trees and undergrowth. Every now and then they could hear faint conversation, and they knew that there must be more soldiers nearby.

At last, towards mid-day, they had almost reached the town. Exhausted, they all lay down to rest, and fell asleep.

* * *

Monday 27th May

Today the rebels were given something to eat. Some of the women attempted to kill one of the Allies by luring him into the village hall, then tying him up and threatening to cut off his head, but his comrades came to the rescue and restored order. Two of the perpetrators, a woman in her fifties and a teenage girl, were hanged from a tree in the village square. The General reminded everyone that it was necessary to take such measures as these people were very dangerous and capable of anything.

Later, the elderly were taken to a field until such a time when they can later be re-settled elsewhere. The Allies have set up their headquarters in a rather charming house, but unfortunately there are no such things as telephones here, nor any mobile phone frequency. Written messages have to be passed by hand to the next town, which the Allies have already succeeded in securing.

* * *

Mark awoke suddenly, and for a split second he thought that he was back in his bedroom. Then he remembered that he was out on the mountainside, facing the town. Beside him lay his three sleeping companions. He began to worry that they had slept for too long, and he thought about everybody back at the village, waiting for help. Then, above his head, he heard a low chuckle. Instantly he sat up and saw crouching behind him a man of about forty-five years of age, with a weathered face and a gun resting across his knees.

"Hello my friend", he said. "Sleep well?"

It was clear that he was not from the army that had invaded the village, but still there was something slightly menacing about him.

Mark turned to his companions: "Jack, Samuel, wake up!"

They awoke, and as they did so, two more men with guns appeared, both slim, with worn, unshaven faces. Peter also awoke and sat up in alarm, confused. The first man spoke, addressing Mark.

"Where are you from?"

"Where are *you* from?" returned Mark.

The man smiled. His eyes creased.

"From that town over there, which has been taken by a foreign army. We don't completely understand their language, but we have heard that they say they have come to bring stability."

"Was your town unstable?" asked Mark.

The man laughed dryly.

"Not before they came, no."

Still uncertain as to whether the man was trustworthy, Mark, in spite of himself, spoke openly.

"We are from a village behind those mountains. The foreign army has taken it over too. They have killed some of our people. We came to try to get help. Can you help us?"

The four friends were led up over the mountain on which they had slept and down the other side, across a small narrow valley to a rocky hillside where there were several caves. Here, they met about thirty men, women and children, all armed. Daniel, the man who had first spoken to Mark, introduced them all. They were a small group, but they were in touch with other groups and they had been planning somehow to recapture the town and drive out the foreign army. They had learned that the whole region was occupied, other towns and villages had been taken over and foreign companies had moved in and bought up various trades, such as mining and silk weaving. Precious items such as paintings, antiques and jewellery had been confiscated, as it was declared that the people now owed the occupiers a lot of money for having been liberated.

Mark and his companions were invited to sit down and have something to eat and drink: some bread, soup and tea. It was clear to everyone just how hungry they were.

"I don't know if the occupiers are going to feed the people in my village. We have to do something quickly", he said anxiously, and he thought of his father and mother, and of Sophia.

Daniel spoke to the company there and sent a message to another group that was living further over in the mountains towards the town. He had a mobile phone, but didn't use it, as calls could easily be intercepted by the occupiers. It was better to send a messenger on foot.

By late afternoon, about sixty men and women, all armed, arrived at the caves. They looked at Mark with curiosity. Some of them recognised Samuel, and went forward to greet him with smiles and warm handshakes. A plan was discussed about how they would take back the village. They were not as heavily armed, nor as numerous as the occupiers, so they would have to be smart.

Jack had never seen so many weapons and wondered from where they had got them all. Daniel told them that a resistance movement was growing, and weapons were being smuggled in, actually from arms dealers who were also supplying the occupiers.

"Money talks", he said.

They had only had a few weeks to learn to fight and most of them had never handled a gun before, but they were becoming increasingly confident. The plan they devised was that they would go back to the village after dark and attempt to retake it. They would have to be invisible, fire at the enemy from long range and use silencers. If necessary, they would take hostages and use them to demand that the occupiers leave.

* * *

Tuesday 28th May

It was discovered yesterday evening that several rebels had escaped. Some of the men were taken out into the village square, stripped naked and put into stress positions for several hours in an attempt to get them to inform the Allies of the whereabouts of the escapees. One of them spat at an Allied soldier and so it was necessary to separate him from the others. He had a hood placed over his head and was taken to an outhouse. I heard a number of screams, but apparently the Allies were unable to get him to cooperate. The Allies were on the alert that day for an attack by insurgents, but all was quiet.

I sat with General Devere and asked him whether he ever thought that it would be possible to establish democracy in this Godforsaken part of the world. He said it would take years, rather than months, as the people were incapable of being given any positions of trust and the area might again slide back into the Middle Ages and cause problems for the Allied administration. I pondered upon the great mission that the Allies had taken upon themselves in order to enlighten the world.

* * *

Daniel led the armed groups towards the village. Only twice were they confronted by soldiers who heard them coming; confrontations which they managed to eliminate immediately, without any sound. They crept back the way that Mark and his companions had escaped; only this time, when they finally arrived at the field at the back of the stable, they found that now a group of soldiers was standing on guard. Daniel ordered ten of his comrades to line up, which they quickly did, bowed on one knee, guns carefully aiming at their target. Then he ordered them to fire, and the soldiers on guard fell to the ground like puppets with their strings cut. Steadily, step by step, the armed groups moved in, quickly taking hostages so that the occupiers would think twice before killing their enemy.

As he lay half-asleep upstairs in the charming house in which he now lived, General Devere suddenly heard a commotion outside, but before he could even look out of the window to see what was going on, two armed men burst into his room, and pushed him at gun point down the stairs, out of the house, all the way to the village square, where the bodies of Sophia and her mother were still hanging, Sophia now only wearing her blouse and, oddly enough, her shoes. Her blouse was torn in two at the front. Her face, arms and legs were bruised, as were those of her mother. Peter had gone to find a ladder so that the bodies could be cut down, as Mark sat on the ground beneath Sophia's shadow, his face hidden in his hands as he sobbed.

* * *

Thursday 30th May

I write this on my way back to the capital, after a disastrous turn of events. The night before last, I was awoken by the sound of gunfire. Before I knew it, an insurgent had burst into my room, grabbed me by the arm and marched me down into the street, where a number of Allied soldiers were being held hostage. I was taken to the village square, where I found insurgents everywhere, brandishing their weapons, their faces hidden with cloths. At that moment, I was prepared to die. I waited to be shot, or to feel the blade of a knife against my throat, but after several hours I realised that that was not going to happen, especially when they allowed me to go to the lavatory, albeit accompanied as far as the lavatory door.

They had discovered my notes and realised that I must be a reporter. I prepared, then, to be interrogated under torture. Instead, I was blindfolded and led back across the mountains. We arrived on the outskirts of the town which the Allies had liberated just two weeks before, and there I was left. Before I had even managed to take off my blindfold, the insurgents had disappeared.

I rushed back to the town, where I found some Allied soldiers who were able to help me. I had to get back to the capital to see my colleagues again and to file my reports. The Allies helped me to find some transport and provided me with a guard, as they said that the country was just too dangerous at that time for me to go anywhere alone, especially as I am a woman. As we drove away from the town this morning, my guard expressed his amazement that the rebels had let me go free. I informed him that it had only been

on condition that I tell the world the truth about
what is happening here.

The Prophet's Birthday

In which a jolly day was had by all...

"Darling", Jeremy called out, putting down his newspaper, "they've just reported the arrest of another chap suspected of terrorist activities. Awful business this..."

His wife, known affectionately as Biddy, was in the hall, arranging a beautiful bunch of roses which she had just picked from the garden.

"Well", she called back, "our noble Prophet, peace and blessings be upon him, has mentioned all the signs. Don't be too downhearted. Remember that Imam Mahdi will bring justice in the end."

"Yes, but in the meantime, all these chaps keep getting arrested", said Jeremy gloomily.

He got up from his armchair and went out of his study, to where Biddy was putting the finishing touches to the bunch of roses.

"There", she said brightly. "Aren't they lovely?"

"Splendid", replied Jeremy. "Our Prophet's favourite flower, and you can understand why."

He bent to inhale their scent.

"Aaah, what a perfect reminder of Heaven."

They had already arranged the great hall in preparation for the *mawlid*, the celebration of the Prophet's birthday. A large tapestry which had been in the family since the fourteenth century was hung across the room, so that men and women could sit separately when they arrived. Carpets were laid out and cushions were placed around the walls, for those who needed to lean back. Incense, brought from Zanzibar by one of their friends, was gently burning in different places throughout the manor house, calming the heart and inspiring the imagination. Tall, glass jugs of freshly-squeezed lemonade were placed on wooden trays painted with flowers, and about forty glasses were arranged next to one another. Homemade shortbread and biscuits sprinkled with lavender were laid out on large plates and covered with glass lids to keep them fresh. The prayer room, next to the great hall, had been cleaned from top to bottom, extra prayer rugs and *tasbih*s brought in, and again, another tapestry hung so that men and women could pray separately in private.

"That Martin Shamus has been writing about Muslims again", said Jeremy. He tended to worry more than Biddy and always mentioned what was on his mind. "Says that when we were confronted with modernity we took a wrong turn."

"Well", said Biddy, "I must say I can't figure out all the nobs on the new washing machine, if that's what he means."

"No, I think he means that we still live as if we're in the Middle Ages."

"Oh", said Biddy, thinking of the fourteenth century tapestry hanging in the great hall. "Golly, that's not very nice is it?"

"And he means that we still do things in the traditional way, same as we've always done for centuries."

"Oh", said Biddy again, thinking about the lavender-sprinkled biscuits, which were an Elizabethan recipe, passed down by her ancestors.

"Still", shrugged Jeremy, "I suppose the poor chap has to earn his crust somehow. You've got to feel sorry for him really."

"Yes", said Biddy thoughtfully. "Poor thing. Probably doesn't know any better. It all goes back to how one's brought up. Manners and all that."

"Yes. Manners are everything", replied Jeremy. "Oh look, here comes Dicky, our first guest."

Dicky was an old friend of the family, who had known Jeremy since they were at *madrasah* together. He now taught Islamic law at Oxford University and gave *tajwīd* lessons for the younger ones who were still learning Qur'an. His footsteps crunched over the gravel drive as he approached the open doorway. He caught sight of Jeremy and Biddy and lifted his hand in greeting.

"*Salaam alaykum*", he called out.

Jeremy went to greet him.

"*Wa alaykum salaam wa rahmatUllah*, brother. So good to see you. How are you?"

"Well, *al-hamdulillah*. It's a beautiful day, isn't it? I can hear the birds singing so loudly in your garden."

"Since we've planted those trees around the tennis court, it really seems to have tranformed things", said Jeremy. "They've all got their little nests in the branches. I'll have to show you later."

"*Salaam alaykum* Dicky", said Biddy.

"*Wa alaykum salaam* sister Biddy. I pray you are in good health and *iman*."

"*Al-hamdulillah*", replied Biddy, graciously inclining her head. "Jeremy, why don't you take Dicky into the great hall, and give him a glass of lemonade? You must be thirsty brother Dicky. It's quite a walk from Little Mead to here, isn't it?"

"A glass of lemonade would be wonderful. *Jazaki Allah khayr*", said Dicky, and Jeremy took him into the great hall, where they sat talking over glasses of lemonade, until the next guests arrived.

"Have you seen that new art installation down at the Tate Modern, Jerry?"

"Not yet. Any good?"

"Worth going to. A reconstruction of the nine celestial spheres and how they relate to the inner and outer senses."

"That must have taken some thinking out."

"Yes, I think the artist is pretty clever. Wish I had her talent."

Just then, the Hirstwood-Brown family arrived, and as Biddy was doing her *'asr* prayer, Jeremy went to greet them: Edward Hirstwood-Brown, his wife Margaret and their five children, three girls and two boys. They were followed by Marcus MacElvoy, his wife Daisy and their four children: three boys and one girl. After that was Bob and Hilda from down the road. They were a sweet elderly couple who helped out at the local mosque on Fridays. Hilda did the flowers and Bob did counselling for the troubled youth. Everybody loved him and called him 'Uncle Bob'. The children ran up to him shouting "Uncle Bob! Uncle Bob!", and flinging his arms open, a high-pitched whistle coming from the gap in his front teeth, he shouted back, "Bob's your uncle!"

"*Salaam alaykum* Uncle Bob!" Jeremy joined in, with great delight.

"*Wa alaykum salaam* brother Jerry. How's it going? Everything all right?"

"*Al-hamdulillah.* Come in, come in."

Bob and Hilda were taken into the great hall and given glasses of lemonade, while more guests arrived: Tony and Barbara, who had come all the way from Banbury; Henry Laughton with his two wives and seven children – Henry in one car with five children, Linda and Anisa in another car with the remaining two. There was Imam Mohamed Cisse from Mali, a sprightly scholar of ninety-three years old, swinging his walking stick in circles, Musa Jahangeer from Mauritius, Lily and Daoud from Spain, Umm Hani from Germany, Sister Khadijah from East London, with her beautiful and intelligent daughter Rabia, and many others, until the hall was full of people drinking lemonade and eating biscuits. Others had adjourned briefly to the prayer room to do their *'asr* prayer, before the event was to begin.

As the afternoon sun turned from pale to golden yellow, Shaykh Haydar Fitzwilliam arrived to give his speech. Jeremy greeted him with warm handshakes and took him into the great hall, inviting him to sit on a chair covered with cushions at the front, so that he was facing everybody. The noise of chatter and laughter was hushed, and two of the brothers began the occasion by sending blessings on the Prophet and his family. They intoned with beautiful, melodic voices and concluded with thanks to the Divine. Then Sister Khadijah's daughter Rabia stood up to recite a poem she had written. She went to the microphone next to where Shaykh Haydar was sitting, tapped it, blew into it, took a deep breath and then began.

I long for my Prophet,
The one who came as a mercy.
O Prophet! I miss you!
Today is your birthday.

Today we remember
How you came to this world.
Your light shone from your eyes,
Your face shone like a pearl.

You asked us to be kind
And gentle to our mothers,
To treat people well
And to be generous to others.

You asked us to be humble
Not rude or proud,
To live a life that is simple,
Not flashy or loud.

We pray to meet you
At the Pool of Kawthar,
With light on our faces
And purified hearts.

O Prophet, I greet you,
Today is your birthday
May Allah send His blessings
To you and your family.

Everyone sent blessings on the Messenger and
his family, and Rabia went to sit down. Then it
was time for Shaykh Haydar Fitzwilliam to give
his talk.   He coughed, and brought the
microphone close. Everyone in the village had
known him for years. He had studied under the
great teachers of Mauritania, Yemen and Ireland.

He taught contemplative techniques which transmitted divine energy into the heart, transforming the consciousness, filling it with love, and when he talked, he exuded an energy which made everyone feel tranquil. Although he was over seventy years old, he looked ten years younger and was always smiling.

"*Bismillah al-Rahman al-Rahīm. Wa as-salāt wa as-salām 'ala Sayyidina al-Mursalīn, wa 'ala ālihi, wa sahbihi, wa sallam.* All praise is due to the One, Who exists beyond the seventy thousand veils of perception, the First Cause, the only Reality, the source of all Knowledge, the source of all Mercy, who brought us into being in order that we may taste His beauty and reflect His attributes. May we overcome the darkness of pride and the smallness of egotism, and surrender ourselves to His Light.

"Today is the day that the Messenger was sent to this world from the realm of the unseen, in order to remind us that we are here only for a short time, and that we have a purpose other than seeking to satisfy our lower desires, or being dazzled by the glitter of material things. Our purpose is to be come conscious of what it is to be a human being; of what our existence actually is and how we relate to the Divine entity that brought us into existence. The Messenger traced a path that brings us back to who we really are. It is in returning to our primordial state that we find peace. It is in being in a state of peace that we can help to beautify the world.

"We must not forget either, that the Messenger brought a philosophy of hope. In this day and age, we know that sickness in the soul affects all of us. Not only that, but external forces are intent on dehumanising us, to justify their inhuman treatment of us, but above all, we must not become victims. It is not only we who are being targetted by malevolent forces – it is also the poor, worldwide. Therefore, we do not battle against these malevolent forces just to save ourselves, but on behalf of everyone who is experiencing injustice. We cannot be strong if we see ourselves as weak. We cannot act if we see ourselves as helpless. Remember that the Messenger said, 'Even if you are at the end of time and planting a seed, finish planting it.' We do not work for immediate results. We should not give up hope just because our effort does not seem to bear the fruit that we want. We must remember that the struggle is ongoing – both within ourselves and in the world. It is important to act, to engage with the world in a way that enhances its beauty and brings it light.

"If we are struck by adversity, we should say *inna lillahi wa inna ilayhi raji'ūn*: we belong to Allah and to Allah we return. What does that mean? It means that Allah is with us and it means that, after all the tribulations, we will return to Allah again, so why be sad? Why be downhearted? We already have the gift of this way of life; we already know how to purify the soul, how to gain knowledge and what is the real

Reality. We know what our existence is rooted in. We are not lost, so why be sad?"

At that moment a breeze blew through the manor house, making the doors and windows slam, and the curtains waft restlessly. A smell of musk drifted through the great hall, and everybody inhaled it. Outside echoed the laughter of children, yet there were no children outside. Above Shaykh Haydar's head flashed a blue and white light. Everyone in hall was encircled by a feeling of well being. Shaykh Haydar continued:

"We are not disconnected from the Divine entity, nor are we disconnected from the ones we love and who love us: our Prophet and the saints of all the ages. The reality of this world is just a thin covering over a realm that is timeless and without dimension, in which the spirit is free. Externally there may be oppression in this world, but internally we are free of all oppression."

As Shaykh Haydar talked, sunlight illuminated the windows of the great hall, and shone on those who were present, even though the sun itself had moved round to the back of the house. A bird trilled a joyful song. By the time that Shaykh Haydar had finished his speech, everyone in the great hall felt that they had some insight into how they could be as ideal human beings, clear souls journeying through this realm, windows through which the sun could shine. Shaykh Haydar concluded his speech with a *du'a*, a request for Allah.

"*Yā* Allah, increase our hearts in knowledge and increase our spirits in strength. Purify us, so that we may realise our humanity more deeply. Help us to follow in the path of your noble Messenger, peace and blessings be upon him and his family, in being in harmony with the Light, in manifesting Your attributes, in healing this world of its pain and conflict, so that we may appreciate the gift of this life which you have bestowed upon us. Salutations to Your Messenger, his family, his companions and the righteous ones who followed after them. May we be worthy of their company. *Ameen.*"

After that, the two brothers who had intoned blessings at the beginning of the ceremony intoned blessings again. On the instructions of Shaykh Haydar, they then led a group *dhikr*, remembrance of Allah. This began with *la ilaha illallah*, to be recited one hundred times. The brothers began, and everyone followed, so that the great hall was filled to the ceiling with the reverberating words: the negation, *la ilaha* – there is no deity; then the affirmation, *illallah* – except the Deity.

As Jeremy recited it, he felt himself disappearing into the Divine. The words lifted him up, high above the floor. He was suspended in mid-air. He wasn't Jeremy anymore: he was a nameless soul, a tiny disembodied glow of consciousness. Biddy, too, felt the power of the words, and felt that everything else reflected their power: the roses in the vase; the apples and pomegranates of the old fourteenth century tapestry; the clouds gathering in the sky; the skylarks. For Bob, the Deity was an old friend, always with him, so he mentioned the words out of love for a good mate. Hilda mentioned them with respect, because she knew it wouldn't be too long before she would have to face the Unknown.

When Imam Mohamed Cisse said them, he was instantly taken back to his childhood in Mali, where he and his family used to gather under the night sky to do *dhikr* until dawn, when the darkness of the sky would split open to let out a trickle of reddish light. For Musa Jahangeer, the words made him think about his smallness in the universe. Here he was, sitting on a tiny planet in space, where someone, somewhere else on that planet, was most likely also reciting *la ilaha illallah*. And he went through all the countries in his mind where people had those words in their mind or on their lips: Mexico, Guyana, United States, Canada, Sweden, Norway, Denmark, Britain and all the European countries, the Caucasus, Russia, China, all the countries in the top half of the African continent, South Africa, the East African islands, Central Asia, the Middle East, Pakistan and India, the South East Asian countries: Thailand, Burma, Malaysia, Indonesia, the Philippines, then down to Australia and New Zealand, then up again to Japan.

The *dhikr* came to an end, and then a group of brothers and sisters commenced a series of *qasīdah*s, songs of love for the Prophet, two sisters beating drums and three brothers reciting the *qasīdah*s in beautiful, unearthly voices. They conveyed something of the spirit of the Prophet and a sweet mood settled over the crowd.

When the *qasīdah*s were over, Shaykh Haydar thanked them, led one last *du‘a*, and then it was time for the food. Everybody moved to sit in rows and long tablecloths embroidered with strawberries were laid out on the floor. Jeremy hurried to the kitchen with Biddy, where their children, Rosy and Jonathan, had been since morning, helping their cook to prepare the lamb, the roast potatoes, the parsnips and the beans. Jeremy had had to have two lambs slaughtered, while Biddy and Rosy had picked the vegetables from the kitchen garden at the back of the manor, where Sam, their gardener, had indicated they were ready. Two stacks of plates stood on the large kitchen table, and Biddy rushed to fill the empty jugs with more lemonade.

As fast as they possibly could, Rosy and Jonathan put the food on the plates, and Jeremy put them on a trolley, wheeling it across to the great hall, where the plates were handed out, each person passing them on to the one before, until everybody had their share. A lively racket filled the house, and Biddy felt a sense of satisfaction. She watched her children and felt proud of them. Jonathan was due to get married next year and Rosy had just got her PhD in microbiology. Biddy had done her best to bring them up according to the Qur'an and Sunnah, which was

94

not easy in this day and age, what with the difficulty of finding a job for someone with a beard and the growing hatred for anyone in a *hijāb*. Just the other day a man had called Rosy 'Osama bin Laden' and said that she should go back to her own country, but Rosy informed the man that she was in fact English, from an old, illustrious aristocratic family that was related to King Henry the Seventh. Rosy then asked if the man could trace his family back that far, at which the man simply stared at her. Rosy could be a little spirited at times. She did not leave it at that. She began to quiz the man about his knowledge of English literature.

No the man could not remember in which year John Milton had written *Paradise Lost*. No he did not know in which Shakespeare play the words 'All's well that ends well' appeared. Rosy moved on to art: no the man did not know why the Expressionist movement had arisen after the First World War; nor did he know why Turner had been so ahead of his time. Rosy was just about to move on to the next subject, by asking the man which Greek philosopher had been the prototype for Newton, when the man, looking a bit flustered, suddenly hurried off.

Jonathan did not deal with things in quite the same way. He had been asked how many times a week he beat his wife. Of course he had said, "I don't know I'm not married yet." When one of his colleagues said loudly that all Muslims should be deported, he piped up, "Please deport me to the Seychelles. They've got some beautiful beaches there." The cook, Mrs Cheeseman, always said, "Jonathan is such a one."

Still, today Biddy put these things out of her mind. She was happy to be feeding the guests and to hear the lively talk. Once she and Jeremy had made sure that everybody had a plate of food and enough lemonade, they themselves sat down to eat, as did Rosy and Jonathan. The lamb was cooked with thyme, and the roast potatoes were done perfectly golden. There was even more than enough gravy to go round.

When everyone had eaten, Jeremy, Biddy, Rosy and Jonathan cleared up the plates, and then it was time for dessert: fruit salad with organic strawberry icecream. The next major operation began, with Rosy and Jonathan filling up the bowls and handing out spoons as fast as possible, and Jeremy wheeling the trolley over to the great hall, where they were handed out. One of the brothers who had sung a *qasīdah* earlier began a spontaneous and beautiful recitation of a poem in praise of the blessings of the Divine, and everyone was filled with joy.

As the sun began to set, and the room darkened, Jeremy switched on the lamps. They were antique and made of engraved glass, so that the light shone softly over everybody's heads. The bowls were cleared away, and it was time to pray. Dicky called the *adhan* and everybody went and assembled in the prayer room next door, where the incense from Zanzibar swirled up to a ceiling painted with stars and calligraphic patterns spelling the name of Allah and Muhammad. The room was silent, except for Dicky doing the *iqamah*, and everybody waited for Shaykh Haydar Fitzwilliam to lead. Shaykh Haydar raised his hands and in a resonant voice, uttered the primordial words *Allahu akbar*.

* * *

"That was such a lovely day, wasn't it Jerry", said Biddy, as they stood together on the lawn, looking up at the stars.

"Really delightful. It just raises one's spirits."

"Yes, it does. We are so fortunate, aren't we?"

"Yes we are, truly. And you know something my dear?"

"What dearest?"

"A strong feeling came into my heart tonight, during Shaykh Haydar's speech, that everything is going to be all right."

"Of course it is, darling", said Biddy. "Everything is going to be all right."

InshaAllah

Glossary

amamah
turban

'asr
afternoon, or afternoon prayer

adhān
call to prayer

al-hamdulillah
all praise is for God

Ash-hadu an-lā ilāha illallahu, wa ash-hadu anna Muhammad Rasulullah
'I witness that there is no god by God and I witness that Muhammad is the Messenger of God': The Muslim declaration of faith.

ayat al-kursī
the Verse of the Throne from the Qur'an, used for protection before embarking on a journey.

barzakh
the intermediary space between the material realm and the divine realm.

Bismillah al-Rahman al-Rahim
In the name of God, the Compassionate, the Merciful

Bismillah
'In the name of God', usually uttered when commencing an action.

dhikr
the mentioning, or remembrance, of God

dhikrullah
the mentioning of God's name

dhu'l-hijja
the month of Hajj

du'a
supplication

fajr
dawn

hijab
headscarf

iman
faith

inna lillahi wa inna ilayhi raji'ūn
'Indeed we belong to God and to Him we return'

InshaAllah
If God wills

iqamah
announcement that the prayer is to start

Jazaki Allah khayr
'May God reward you with goodness' (here, spoken to a woman)

jubba
long overgarment

khanqah
place of retreat and spiritual training

madrasah
religous college

majlis
a meeting, or gathering

mawlid
birthday

nafs
soul, or ego.

qasīdah
song of praise for the Prophet

ruku'

the bow in the prayer that comes before the prostration

SallAllahu alayhi wa ālih
'Peace be upon him and his family.'

sayyid
a descendent of Prophet Muhammad

sujūd
prostration

tajwīd
the science of correct pronunciation of the Qur'an

tasbih
prayerbeads, or a collection of praises for God

Wa alaykum salaam wa rahmatUllah
And to you peace and the mercy of God

Wa as-salāt wa as-salām 'ala Sayyidina al-Mursalīn, wa 'ala ālihi, wa sahbihi, wa sallam
And greetings and peace upon the Master of all the Messengers, and upon his family, and companions, and blessings.

zakāt
obligatory charitable tax to purify of one's wealth